P9-AOU-270

The Cat who Lost his Purr

MICHELE COXON

Star Bright Books
New York

Bootle woke one morning
without his purr.
His house was quiet and empty.

'Where is my purr?' wondered
Bootle, who was normally happy
and contented.
He washed and thought hard.
'When did I have it last?'
But like all cats he was not very
good at remembering yesterday.

He didn't know about things like 'tomorrow', or the names of the days of the week.

Or even that the world was round. To him it was flat, and today it was purrless.

The things he knew were useful, like if it was a wet fur day or a dry fur day.

Or what time his tins were opened and when his milk was poured.

'I will go and find my purr,' decided Bootle and he set off.

Bootle started by looking in the
bathroom.
DRIP, DRIP, DRIP, DROP,
went the tap.

'Is this my purr?'
No, the wet drip sound was not
his purr.
'Is my purr down here?'
No, it was not in the place where
his unfurry friends sometimes sat.

Bootle heard a
sound very
like his purr.

BUZZ, BUZZ, BUZZ.

'Is this my purr?'
No, it was just a fly, so he ate it.
'Where did the noise go?'
wondered Bootle, licking his lips.

He went downstairs to the kitchen where there were lots of interesting sounds.

HUMM, HUMM, HUMM.

The fridge hummed softly and it smelt good. Bootle was a clever cat, he knew how to open the fridge and look inside.
'Is my purr here?'
'No, not even inside the sausages,' thought Bootle, feeling rather full.

There was a sound from under the cupboard.

SCRATCH, SCRATCH, SCRATCH, SQUEAK.

'That sound could be my purr.'
But the scratch, squeak ran
away from his fine, sharp claws.

A pleasant TICK, TICK, TOCK,
came from the clock.
'Could that be my purr?' he
                    wondered.

Bootle climbed up but a yellow
bird knocked him down with a
loud 'Cuckoo!'
'Meow!' yelled Bootle.

In the laundry
room the
washing
monster made
lots of loud, wet
gurgling noises.

SWISH, SWISH, SWASH.

'Is my purr having a wash?'
Bootle thought a cat thought
(which isn't very long)
and looked until his whiskers
felt dizzy.
'No, my purr is not there.
It hates getting wet.'

In the sitting room the fish blew
bubbles at him from their watery
world.

BUBBLE, BUBBLE, BUBBLE.

Bootle didn't like getting his
paws wet either so he could not
find out if the fish
had his purr. He
turned away
sadly.

'My purr must be outside in the sunshine. It loves the warm sun,' thought Bootle. But he had to chase away some naughty blue tits who were stealing his milk.

CRASH!

A thrush looked as if it might
be banging his poor purr on
a stone.

CRACK, CRACK, CRACK.

Bootle rushed to the rescue.
But it was only an unhappy snail
which crawled away without
saying thank you.
Cats appreciate good manners.
Snails are always
miserable and
never smile.

Bootle went back to the house
in a down-tail mood.
Cats don't cry because that
makes them wet.
'Poor me,' sighed Bootle.
He had a drink of milk, to help
him think, and licked all the
chocolate off some biscuits just
for comfort.

And then he heard a sound. Lots
of sounds, coming into the house.
Voices of his two-legged unfurry
friends.

'My openers of
cans.'
'My pourers of
cream.'
'My strokers of fur.'
They were home and
they had found his purr.
He purred with joy.

PURR, PURR, PURR,
PURR, PURR.

At last his life (which to a cat means today) was purr-fect. He was the most contented cat in the whole flat garden of his world and would be until the end of his whiskers.

And now his tale is told.

In memory of Karen, and for her husband Charlie and their children
Ben, Katy and Becky

Text and illustrations copyright © 1991 Michele Coxon

This edition published 2000 by Happy Cat Books, Bradfield, England and in the
United States of America by Star Bright Books, New York

ISBN 1-887734-77-5

Printed in Hong Kong by Wing King Tong Co. Ltd.

9 8 7 6 5 4 3 2 1